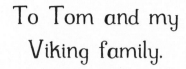

To Tom and my
Viking family.

Thanks to my editors Emily Ford
and Justine Smith
and to my designer Lorna Scobie.

First published 2019 by Macmillan Children's Books
an imprint of Pan Macmillan
The Smithson, 6 Briset Street, London EC1M 5NR
EU representative: Macmillan Publishers Ireland Ltd, 1st Floor,
The Liffey Trust Centre, 117-126 Sheriff Street Upper,
Dublin 1, D01 YC43
Associated companies throughout the world
www.panmacmillan.com

(HB) ISBN: 978-1-0350-2306-6

Text and illustrations copyright © Marta Altés 2019

The right of Marta Altés to be identified as author and illustrator of this work
has been asserted by her in accordance with the Copyright, Designs and Patents Act 1988.

9 8 7 6 5 4 3 2 1

A CIP catalogue record for this book is available from the British Library.

Printed in China

MIX
Paper | Supporting
responsible forestry
FSC® C116313
FSC
www.fsc.org

marta altés

FIVE MORE MINUTES

MACMILLAN CHILDREN'S BOOKS

Time is a funny thing.
Dad talks about it a lot.
But I think I know
more about time than he does.

That's why every morning I'm in charge
of letting him know when . . .

. . . it's TIME TO WAKE UP!

Dad always asks for
'just five more minutes'.

He thinks five minutes isn't very long.
But that's not true.

Five minutes is
a long time.

Look how much we can get done!
We can even make Dad's breakfast.

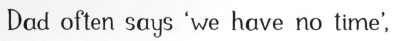

Dad often says 'we have no time',

but that makes no sense.

We always have time!
Time for puddles . . .

...and time to make new friends.

Time to juggle,

and time to watch the birds.

See? I know more about time than Dad.

He often gets confused about time.

Dad thinks an hour is a long time, but that's not true.

One hour isn't very long.

We've only just started playing!

And Dad ALWAYS says 'it's time to go'...

... when clearly, it's NOT!

Time often surprises Dad.

But this never happens to me.

I always know what time it is.

Now it's time to run to swimming . . .

... and – oops! NOW it's time to go home.

See? I know more
about time than Dad.

He doesn't have a clue.
He says 'Dad time is peaceful and quiet'.

But once more he is wrong...

...Dad time is fun and
LOUD!

Dad always says
'time goes very fast'.

But that's not true either

because I know time can go slowly,

especially when we are hungry!

And sometimes,

time goes very

veeeeeery

veeeeeeeery

slooooOOOOOOowly.

I wonder why?

Time is a funny thing,
Dad talks about it a lot.
But even though I know SO much
more about it than him,

every evening, I don't mind
letting him be in charge when . . .

I don't know how, but Dad really does
know a lot about this kind of time.

And I always ask for 'just five more minutes'
because I know exactly how much time that is . . .

. . . lots of time
with Dad.